This Little Tiger book belongs to:

Xander Ashton-Ray Maynard

Summer 2017

For Graduation from nursery

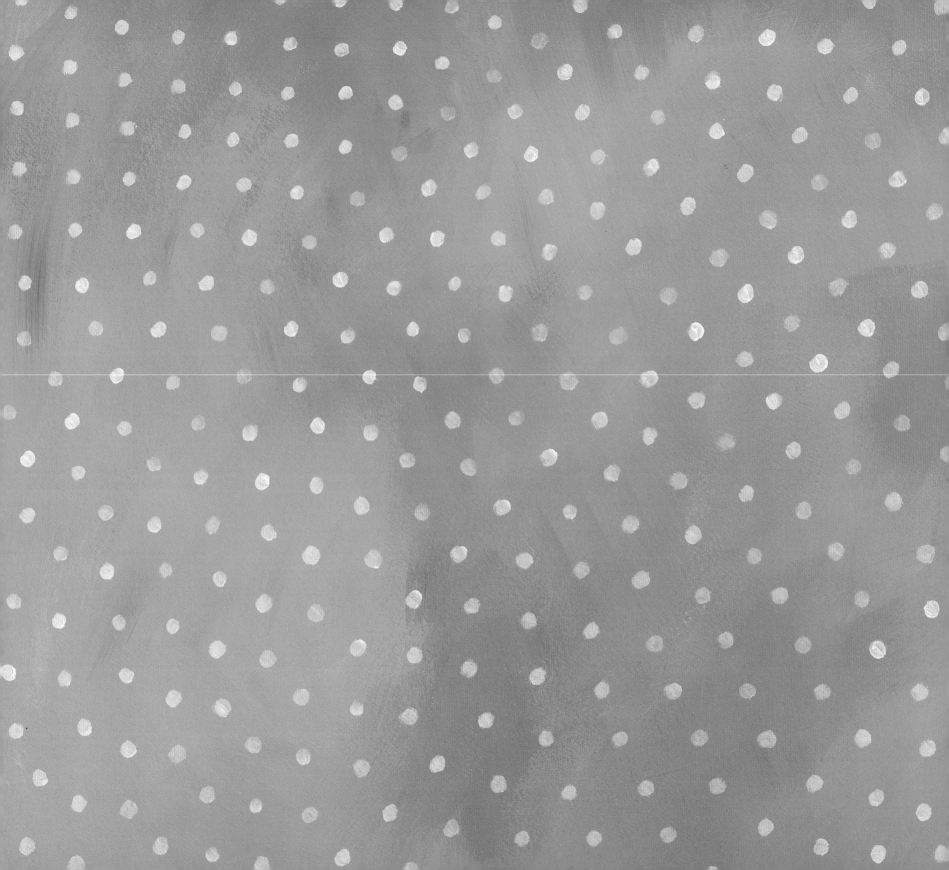

For Matthew, Liz, William, Daniel and Harriet (and White Rabbit) ~ J C

For Martin and Nicola, with love ~ P B

LITTLE TIGER PRESS
1 The Coda Centre, 189 Munster Road,
London SW6 6AW • www.littletiger.co.uk
First published in Great Britain 2008
This edition published 2016
Text copyright © Paul Bright 2008 • Illustrations copyright © Jane Chapman 2008
Visit Jane Chapman at www.ChapmanandWarnes.com
Paul Bright and Jane Chapman have asserted their rights to be identified as the
author and illustrator of this work under the Copyright, Designs and Patents Act, 1988
A CIP catalogue record for this book is available
from the British Library
All rights reserved • ISBN 978-1-84869-388-3
Printed in China • LTP/1900/1740/1216
2 4 6 8 10 9 7 5 3

The Bears
in the Bed
and the
Great
Big
Storm

Paul Bright   Jane Chapman

LITTLE TIGER PRESS
London

How the wind blew!

It howled in the treetops, so that
the branches bent and creaked and the
leaves shivered and shook. It blew over
the hills and the high places, howling and
wailing through the rocky passes.

Bear and Mrs Bear slept warm and
snug and untroubled in their bed.

Then Bear felt a tugging at his blanket. He opened one eye. There was Baby Bear.

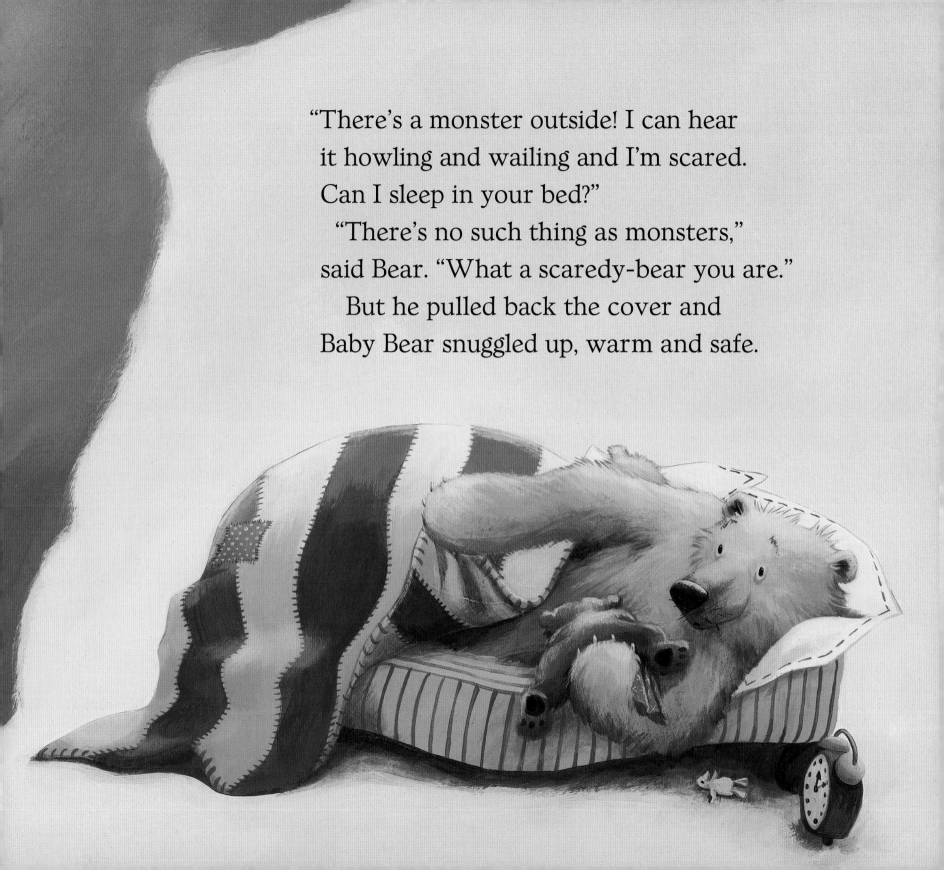

"There's a monster outside! I can hear
it howling and wailing and I'm scared.
Can I sleep in your bed?"
  "There's no such thing as monsters,"
said Bear. "What a scaredy-bear you are."
But he pulled back the cover and
Baby Bear snuggled up, warm and safe.

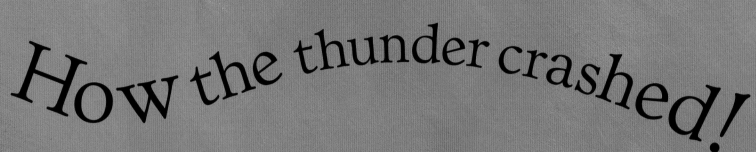

How the thunder crashed!

It boomed and crackled so the house
shuddered and the windows rattled.
It grumbled and rumbled and
echoed and faded, only to
boom and crash again.

Mrs Bear and Baby Bear slept warm and snug and untroubled in their bed. But Bear lay awake, with his paws over his ears.

Then Bear felt a tapping on his shoulder.
There was Little Bear.
"There's a monster outside! Its tummy is
rumbling and grumbling like it's going to
eat me! Can I sleep with you?"

"There's no such thing as monsters," said Bear. "You're another scaredy-bear." But he lifted the cover and Little Bear snuggled up, warm and safe.

How the lightning flashed!

It forked and flickered, lighting the scurrying clouds and splashing quick, black shadows on the windows and the walls.

Mrs Bear and Baby Bear and Little Bear slept warm and snug and untroubled in their bed. But Bear lay awake, with his pillow wrapped around his head.

Then Bear felt a tap on his nose. It was Young Bear. "There's a monster outside! It has huge, twisted horns and it's making shadows on my wall. Can I come and sleep in your bed?"

"There's no such thing as monsters!" cried Bear.
   But he let Young Bear climb into the bed, where he snuggled up, warm and safe.

Now Bear was wide awake.

He listened to the wind howling and the thunder crashing. He watched the lightning fork and flash.

"Young Bear's right," he thought. "The shadows on the wall *do* look like monster horns." And he pulled up the bed covers right over his head.

Suddenly, there was a

RAT-TAT-TAT at the door . . .

Everybody woke at once.
"Wh-wh-who can that be?" said Bear.
"It's probably nothing at all," said Mrs Bear.
"Go and see." And she gave Bear a little push.

Bear climbed nervously out of bed.
He picked up a candle to light his way,
and padded slowly, ever so slowly,
to the door.
   "You're all such scaredy-bears!"
he said to the others. "There's no such
thing as m-m-m-monsters!"

As he turned the
handle, the wind
blew the door open.
The candle went out.
And everything was
black as black.

Then the lightning flashed....

"A MONSTER!" shouted Bear.
He jumped back in fright and dived
straight under the bed.

"It's not a monster, it's a moose!" said Moose, stepping through the doorway. "The storm has blown my house away. Can I sleep in yours?"

Bear peered out from under the bed.

Baby Bear and Little Bear and Young Bear laughed and laughed and laughed.

"What a scaredy-bear you are!" they said. "Don't you know . . .

THERE'S NO SUCH

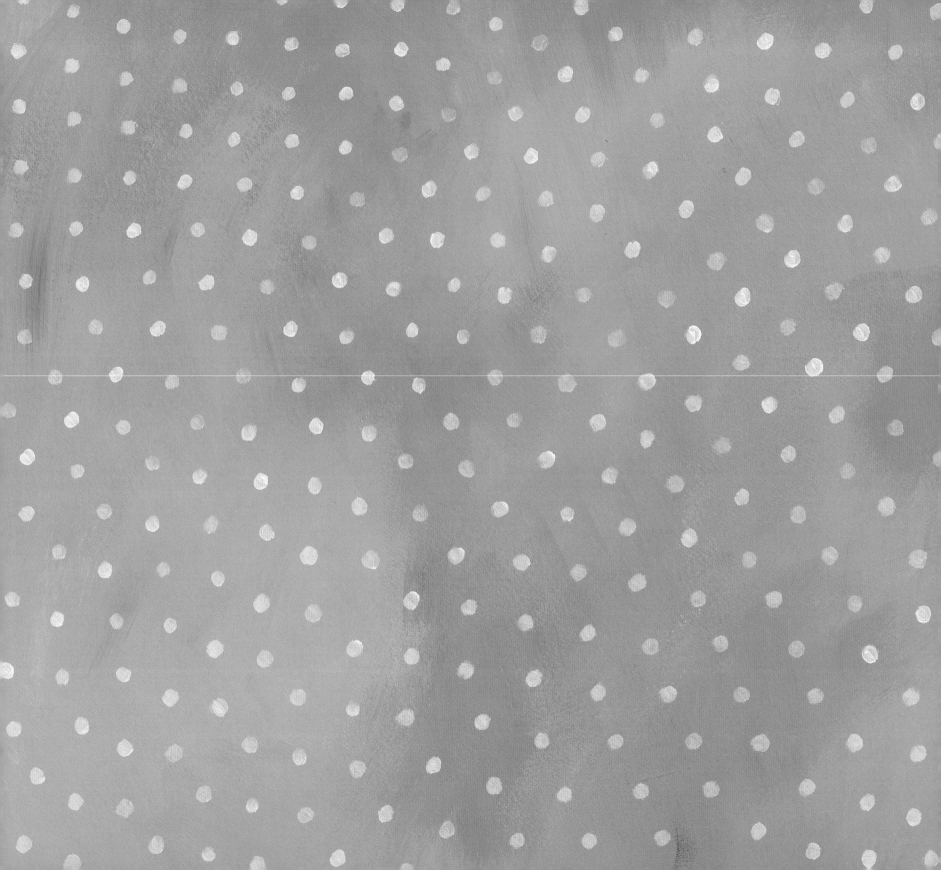

CD track 1 – complete story with original music and sound effects

CD track 2 – story with page turn pings encourages learner readers to join in

Running time – over 15 mins • Produced by Stationhouse and by Matinée Sound & Vision Ltd

Music composed by Sam Park • Text copyright © Paul Bright 2008

Visit our website www.littletiger.co.uk for details of other Little Tiger Picture Book and CD Sets, plus our full catalogue of novelty, board and picture books.